For Sara Donati, who slept one night at my house, and dreamt that I made a book called "Short Stories of the Night" with a pink cover and a handwritten title.

This edition first published in 2018 by Gecko Press
PO Box 9335, Wellington 6141, New Zealand
info@geckopress.com

English-language edition © Gecko Press Ltd 2018

Original title *Sagor om Natten* © Lilla Piratförlaget AB, 2017
Text and illustrations © Kitty Crowther 2017

Distributed in the United States and Canada by Lerner Publishing Group, lernerbooks.com
Distributed in the United Kingdom by Bounce Sales and Marketing, bouncemarketing.co.uk
Distributed in Australia by Scholastic Australia, scholastic.com.au
Distributed in New Zealand by Upstart Distribution, upstartpress.co.nz

Published with the support of the Wallonia-Brussels Federation

FÉDÉRATION
WALLONIE-BRUXELLES

Translated by Julia Marshall, edited by Penelope Todd, typesetting by Katrina Duncan
Printed in China by Everbest Printing Co. Ltd, an accredited ISO 14001 & FSC certified printer
ISBN hardback: 978-1-776571-97-0

For more curiously good books, visit geckopress.com

KITTY CROWTHER

STORIES OF THE NIGHT

Interpreted by Sam McCullen

GECKO PRESS

"Tell me three stories, please, please, please?"
asks Little Bear.

"Three!" says Mother Bear.

"Yes. I said please three times!"

"Which story would you like first?" asks Mother Bear.

"The one that says it's time to go to sleep," says Little Bear.

Mother Bear smiles. "Of course."

IN THE DEEP forest, not too far from here, lived a Night Guardian.

Every evening, just before the moon began to rise, she banged her gong.

Donnnnng Donnnnnnnng

"It's time," said the Night Guardian. "The time when little ones and big ones go to sleep."

"Two more minutes?" begged the fish. "I'm still playing."

"You can leap some more tomorrow,"
said the Night Guardian.

Donnnnng Donnnnnnnng

"It's time to go to bed, little ant."

"I just need to get this one piece of petal,"
called a tiny voice.

"Quickly then. Sleep will be with you soon."

The little ant ran to fetch his petal, and a huge
yawn filled his sweet black face. Then he trotted back
to his underground town.

Donnnnng Donnnnnnnng

"Time for bed, small ermine," said the Night Guardian. "Your mother is so tired."

"I am not tired at all!" complained the ermine.

"Go to bed, and then your sleep will catch you," said the Night Guardian. "Your lovely mother will bring you an egg for breakfast."

"Yum!" called the ermine as she dived into her mother's warm soft fur.

"It's time."

Donnnnng Donnnnnnnng

"The sky is all black now. But we can count on the stars to lead us into tomorrow."

Donnnnng Donnnnnnnng

The Night Guardian went back to her snug little cave. Bed at last! It was her turn now to search for a star to follow across the night sky.

The Night Guardian shot up in bed.

"But who will tell me when it's time to sleep?"

She burst out laughing. Every night, the same thing.

It was time for her secret ritual.

Carefully she took her gong and made the softest, most delicate *donnng* you've ever heard.

She listened for a while.
Then she put away her gong, lay down,
chose a star, and fell asleep.

"The Night Guardian never tells me when it's time for bed,"
says Little Bear. "It's always you who does it."

"That's true," says Mother Bear.

"And now for the second story," says Little Bear.
"The little girl with a sword who gets lost."

IT WAS berry-picking day. Zhora's mother had asked
all of her children to collect red and black berries,
or the dark-blue ones.

Zhora dreamt of finding a dark blackberry.
But in this corner of the forest, there were none.

"I must go further, over by the lakes," she thought with pride.

"I've got you now!" Zhora exclaimed.

She had discovered the most beautiful blackberry in the whole forest. But now she had to find her way home, and she was not at all sure how.

"Where am I?" Zhora asked herself. She'd been going in circles for hours, fighting through brambles, ferns and nettles.

She heard a rustling sound behind her.
Then a branch cracked.

Zhora shot off as fast as her short legs would
carry her, clasping her sword and her basket close.

"That's a pretty sword!" said a familiar voice.

"Oh! It's you, Jacko Mollo!" said Zhora, barely breathing.

"You're a long way from home, Zhora," said Jacko Mollo. "Would you like to come to my tent and share that delectable blackberry?"

"Perhaps," said Zhora, looking at the delicious black fruit.

"We should go soon though," whispered Jacko Mollo. "There's a hungry, grumpy owl close by."

"How big is this owl?" asked Zhora.

Jacko Mollo just stared at Zhora, his eyes wide.

"What are we waiting for!" cried Zhora.

They came at last to Jacko Mollo's pine-branch tent,
at the top of the tallest tree in the forest.

Zhora was not at all dizzy. She was so happy to be there.

"And now, we'll sleep," said Jacko Mollo. After a while he added, "Comfy, huh?"

"Yes…well actually…no," replied Zhora.

Zhora snuggled under a leaf and fell fast asleep.
She felt safe.

At dawn, she heard her brothers and sisters calling
her in the distance. She was so excited to tell them
about her adventures, but her bed was snuggly and
warm so she stayed just a little longer. Right now,
being here was perfect.

"I love blackberries! Almost as much as I love honey!" cries Little Bear. "Could we go and pick some soon?"

"Of course," says Mother Bear. "So, the third story. Which one will it be?"

"The one with the man in a big coat who never sleeps!"

THERE WAS once a little man called Bo who never took off his coat. He lived in a nest that had belonged to a grumpy old owl. Bo had exchanged his small silver watch for the nest.

The owl had left a few feathers for Bo's bed before packing her suitcase and leaving the tree forever.

Every night was the same. Despite the soft feathers, Bo found it impossible to get a wink of sleep.

Bo went out into the woods to look for some sleep. Deep down, he knew that this would take him a while. At least until sunrise.

As Bo reached the shore, he wondered if his friend Otto the otter was still awake, writing poems on stones and throwing them into the sea.

"Still have trouble sleeping?" called Otto.

"Yes," sighed Bo.

Otto turned to the open sea and said, "Why don't you go for a swim?"

"It's far too chilly," grumbled Bo.

"Go in with your coat on then," suggested Otto.

The water sparkled beautifully. Bo stood up, took off his shoes, gave his hat to Otto, and waded into the water.

Otto chuckled.

Bo swam for a while. He felt so happy, and as light as a feather.
Under the water, he found one of his friend's stone poems.

He tucked it into his pocket,
then he swam up to the surface.

As Bo left the sea, he saluted his friend and said,
"You must keep my hat!"

"But it's your best one!" said Otto.

"Don't worry, I have others," said Bo,
and he headed off home.

"Hey, Otto!" Bo called from the distance.
"I found one of your stone poems!"

Otto waved his new hat.

Bo was delighted to be back in his bed.

The moment his head touched the pillow, he sank into a deep sleep. He didn't ask if this was because of his night swim or because he'd found one of Otto's stone poems or because he had such a wonderful friend—or even if it was a mixture of everything.

"He must be happy now," says Little Bear.

"Oh yes," replies Mother Bear.

"I wish I had a stone poem,"
says Little Bear.

"If you like, we can make one tomorrow.
But now, it's time for you to sink into a deep sleep."

Mother Bear kisses Little Bear and whispers,
"Choose a star to lead you into tomorrow."

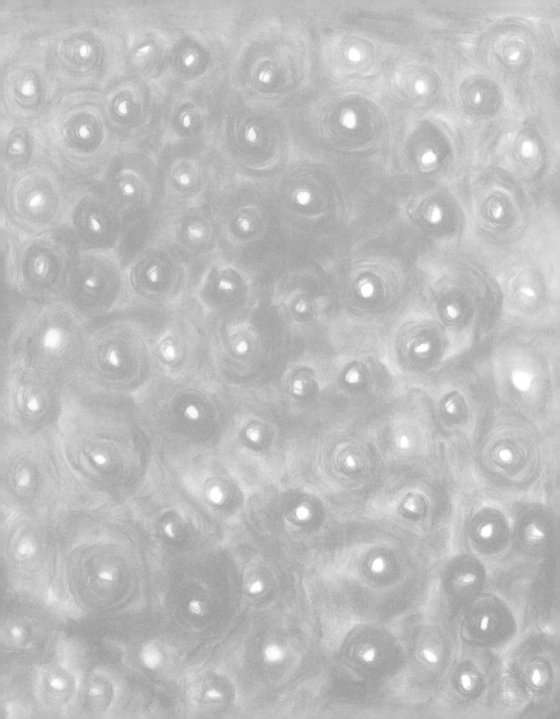